Cara and the Wizard

To Flo and Iris — L. F.
For Delfina and Felipe, with love from Auntie Vale — V. D.

Barefoot Books
294 Banbury Road
Oxford, OX2 7ED

Graphic design by Love Has No Logic Design Group, Chicago, IL
Colour separation by B & P International, Hong Kong
Printed in China on 100% acid-free paper
This book was typeset in Albemarle, Bembo Infant
and Captain Kidd
The illustrations were prepared in
gouache paints and finished digitally

The editors would like to thank Year 2
at St Mary and All Saints School for all
their careful reading.

Sources:
Nic Leodhas, Sorche. 'The Lass
Who Went Out at the Cry of Dawn.'
Thistle and Thyme. New York:
Holt, Rinehart and Winston, 1962.

ISBN 978-1-84686-779-8

British Cataloguing-in-Publication Data:
a catalogue record for this book
is available from the British Library

1 3 5 7 9 8 6 4 2

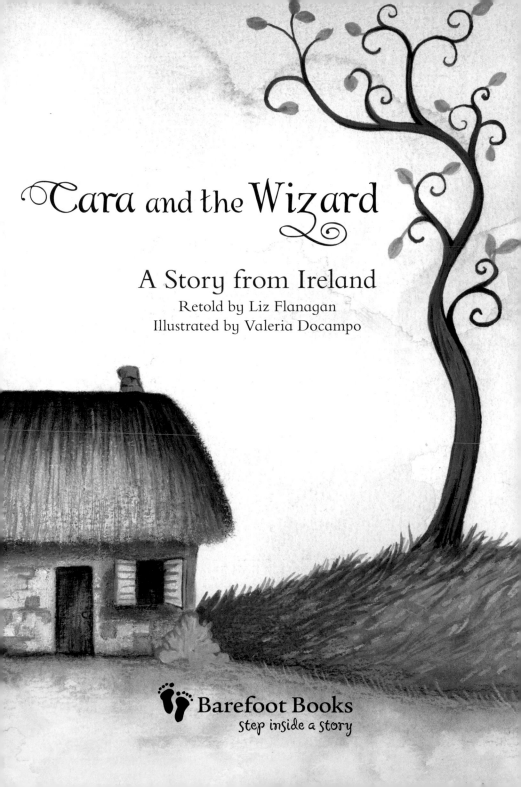

Cara and the Wizard

A Story from Ireland

Retold by Liz Flanagan

Illustrated by Valeria Docampo

Barefoot Books
step inside a story

CONTENTS

CHAPTER 1
The Two Sisters

Long ago in Ireland, there were two
sisters called Molly and Cara. They loved
each other very much. Day and night, they
were always together.

But one morning, Molly went out alone.
She went out at daybreak to wash her
face in the morning dew. She did not come
home again.

Molly's father looked everywhere for
her. Nobody had seen her anywhere. Her
mother cried for days.

Cara missed her sister terribly. Without Molly, she was sad and lonely.

But Cara was brave — and clever too. She said, 'I will go out into the wide world. I will look everywhere until I find Molly.'

She asked her mother and father to wish her luck. Cara's father gave her his blessing and one gold coin. She put it in her purse.

'Take my blessing with you too,' said Cara's mother. 'And here are some gifts from me.'

She gave Cara some pure white wool, a golden needle, a packet of pins, a sharp knife and a silver thimble. 'Keep them safe until you need them,' she told Cara.

Cara set off singing. She knew she had
to find Molly and she was not going to
come home without her.

CHAPTER 2
The Cart with No Horse

Cara walked for days and days. She travelled many long miles.

One day, she met an old lady who told her, 'There is a wicked wizard who lives in a castle at the top of that high hill. Maybe he has taken your sister away.'

Cara walked to the bottom of the high

hill. It was very steep and covered in rocks.

She sat down to rest before she climbed it.

While Cara was resting, a man with a
cart came travelling past. He was a tinker.
He went from place to place selling his
kettles, cups, pots and pans. His cart was
stacked high with all sorts of things made
of metal. The cart went clink! clank! clink!
clank! as it travelled along the road.

But this tinker had no horse. Instead,
he was pulling the cart himself.

So Cara called out, 'That looks like hard work!
Where is your horse?'

'It's hard work, sure enough,' said the tinker.
'But I have no money to buy a horse.'

Cara saw that the tinker looked tired. She felt sorry for him. 'Here, take my purse. I have one gold coin that my father gave me,' she told him gently. 'You need it more than I do. Go and buy yourself a horse.'

The tinker's eyes sparkled with tears. 'Thank you!' he said. 'Nobody else will speak to me, but you have been very kind.'

They sat down and talked together. The tinker asked Cara, 'Where are you going all alone?'

Cara pointed to the castle, towering above them. 'I'm going to look for my sister in the wizard's castle,' she said.

The tinker tried to change her mind. He said, 'Please don't go there! Many go into the castle, but no one comes out again.'

Cara gave a shrug. 'Molly is the only sister I have,' she said. 'I know there may be danger, but I must find her before I go home again.'

So the tinker said, 'I understand. You
are very brave and your sister is lucky to
have you. So, if you must go there, please
remember this:

'Whatever you hear, whatever you see,
Things are never what they seem to be.'

19

And off he went along the road. Clink!

Clank! Clink! Clank!

Cara started to climb the hill.

CHAPTER 3
The Ragged Old Man

When Cara was halfway up the hill,
she sat down under a tree to rest. An old
man dressed in rags came walking past. His
clothes were falling apart. Cara saw that he
had pinned them together with thorns.

Cara said, 'Hello! Would you like these pins? My mother gave them to me. You need them more than I do.'

The old man smiled at Cara. 'Thank you!' he said. 'No one else even looks at me, but you have been very kind.'

He sat down with Cara under the tree and they talked together.

The old man asked, 'Where are you
going all alone?'

Cara pointed to the dark castle
above them. 'I am going there to look
for my sister.'

The old man begged Cara not to go
there. He said, 'That old wizard is wicked.
He will cast a spell on you.'

But Cara said, 'I have to go. I must
rescue my sister!'

So the old man said, 'If you must go
there, then remember this:

'Silver and gold will serve you well.
Silver and gold will break the spell.'

24

Cara thanked the old man dressed in
rags. She left him mending his clothes by the
side of the road.

CHAPTER 4
The Wizard's Castle

At last, Cara climbed to the top of the

hill. She opened the heavy castle gates and

walked in. She marched up to the huge

front door and knocked loudly.

Suddenly, the wizard appeared next to Cara. He wore a swirling black cloak. His eyes were red and his face was white. The wizard glared down at Cara.

'Who are you?' he growled. 'Why do you come knocking on my door?'

Cara said, 'I've come for my sister Molly.

I think she's here and I want her back.'

'Very well,' said the wizard. 'Follow me.'

He took Cara to a room and left her there.

The room was empty. Cara could
not see Molly anywhere. She sat down
to wait. Suddenly, the room was
filled with smoke!

Flames crackled around Cara's feet.

The air was full of thick grey smoke.

'The castle is on fire!' Cara shouted.

She wanted to get up and run away.

Then she remembered what the
tinker had told her and she
whispered the words to herself:

'Whatever you hear, whatever you see,
Things are never what they seem to be.'

'This must be the wizard's magic,'
she thought. So she sat and waited.

Sure enough, the flames and the
smoke vanished all at once.

Next, Cara heard a sound that made her heart break. It was her sister's voice. 'Cara! Help me! Please, help me!' Molly's voice begged.

Cara jumped up. She nearly ran to go and find Molly.

Just in time, she remembered the tinker's
words again:

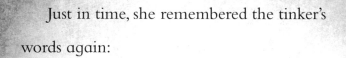

'Whatever you hear, whatever you see,
Things are never what they seem to be.'

'This isn't real. It's only another spell,'
she said to herself. But her feet would not
keep still while Molly's voice cried for her.

So Cara took the pure white wool that her mother had given her and she tied herself to the chair.

At last, the voice stopped calling. Cara took her sharp knife and cut herself free.

The wizard came back. He was very angry when he saw that Cara was still there.

CHAPTER 5

The Hall of Statues

'Come with me,' the wizard said to
Cara. He took her to a grand hall with high
windows. There was nothing in it except for
seven white statues. Each statue looked just
like Molly.

The wizard said to Cara, 'If you can tell
me which one is your sister, then you can
both go free.' He laughed nastily.

Cara walked slowly up and down and
looked at each statue. The wizard watched
from the other side of the great hall.

As she walked, Cara remembered what

the old man in rags had said:

> 'Silver and gold will serve you well.
> Silver and gold will break the spell.'

She took her silver thimble and put it on

the first statue's finger.

The silver thimble turned black as ink.
Cara knew this statue was not her sister. She
tried the thimble on the next statue. Again,
it went black. She did this six times.

Finally, Cara slipped the silver thimble onto the last statue's finger. This time it glowed with a dazzling bright light. The statue's white skin grew warm. Molly stood there, alive and well.

But Cara did not shout out. To trick
the wizard, she stood in front of Molly so he
could not see that her sister was alive again.
And then clever Cara pretended to weep.

The wizard laughed at her tears. While
he was laughing, Cara whispered to Molly,
'Quick! We must leave now.'

Before the wizard could see what had really happened, Molly and Cara fled from the hall.

The two sisters hugged each other. 'You came and found me!' cried Molly. 'But we must be quick, or the evil wizard will catch us both.'

Molly was right. As soon as the wizard noticed that they had gone, he was very angry.

No one had ever escaped from the wizard before. He sent a huge wolf to chase after the sisters.

Cara and Molly ran fast, but the fierce wolf ran faster. It had nearly caught them, when Cara remembered what the old man in rags had said:

'Silver and gold will serve you well.
Silver and gold will break the spell.'

She took out her golden needle. The wolf
jumped up at her, snarling and growling.
Bravely, Cara stabbed the wolf right between
the eyes. The wolf fell down dead at her feet.

The wizard was watching all this from
a tower at the top of his castle. When he
saw what Cara had done, he screeched
with rage. He flew after the sisters, his black
cloak flowing out behind him like wings.

They all got into the coach and rode back to Molly and Cara's home. The sisters' mother and father wept for joy when they saw them.

Cara married the fine young man with the pins. Molly married the tinker with the shining coach.

They all lived happily together for the rest of their days. And the sisters were never parted again.

At the bottom of the hill, they met
a handsome young man with a shining
coach. 'I was the tinker with no horse,' he
said. 'You have freed me from the wizard's
terrible curse.'

As soon as the wizard fell, his great castle crumbled into dust. All of his evil spells had been broken.

Cara and Molly walked slowly down the hill hand in hand. Halfway down, they saw a fine young man. He had Cara's pins in his hands. 'I was the old man you helped,' he said. 'You have freed me from the wizard's spell.'

Cara had nothing left except the sharp
knife and the blessings from her parents.
When the wizard swooped down at them,
Cara threw the knife. The knife flew straight
and strong into the wizard's heart. The wizard
dropped from the sky like a stone.